Bob's Boots

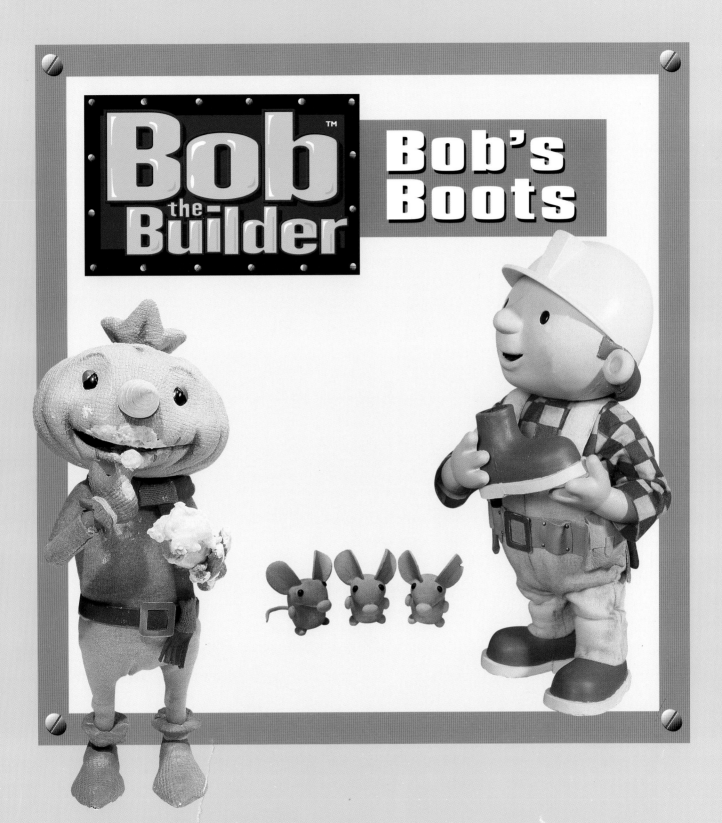

Bob the Builder™

Bob's Boots

HINKLER
BOOKS

One morning a big, brown parcel arrived for Bob. He showed it to Finn.

"Look what came in the mail, Finn," said Bob. "My new boots! What do you think Finn?"

Finn did a back flip in his tank to show how much he liked Bob's new boots. Bob was excited.

"You know, I think I'll wear them to work today," said Bob.

In the yard, Wendy was telling everyone their jobs for the day.

"Er … Lofty you're with Bob today," said Wendy. "He needs you to help fix a broken gate."

Bob rushed out to show them all his new boots. When he walked around, there was a squeaking noise.

"Shhh everyone," said Bob. "I can hear squeaking."

When Bob stopped walking, the squeaking stopped too.

"Uh, I can't hear anything," whispered Muck.

When Bob started walking again, the squeaking noise came back.

"Oh yes, I can hear it now," said Wendy.

"Ha ha! It sounds like mice!" laughed Dizzy.

"OHHHHH," trembled Lofty. "MmmMMICE!"

"Don't worry Lofty. It's not mice," said Wendy.

"Ohh … Oh if … if you're sure," said Lofty, who was frightened of mice.

But they could all hear the squeaking noise when Bob walked around the yard.

"Ha ha ha, Bob I know where the squeaks are coming from," laughed Wendy.

"Where?" asked Bob.

"Your new boots," said Wendy. "They need to be broken in to soften the leather."

"Ha ha! You sound like you need oiling, Bob," Scoop laughed.

"Well, we'd better get some work done," said Bob.

"Can we fix it?" called Scoop.

"YES WE CAN!!!" everyone shouted.

Meanwhile, Spud, Travis, and Farmer Pickles were trying to work out the best way to get to Bob's yard.

"… You see, Travis," said Spud, "the quickest way to Bob's yard is to go left at the fork."

"I'm sure it's right," disagreed Travis.

Bird, who was watching them talking, was starting to get confused.

"Oh well now," said Farmer Pickles. "They say the quickest way is usually as the crow flies. It means the quickest way to get to anywhere is in a straight line."

"I can walk faster than any old bird can fly," said Spud. "Bird, come on, I'll race you to Bob's yard."

Later, on their job, Bob and Lofty tried to lower the gate into place, but a strong wind was blowing it around.

"Left a little. OK ... straight down," said Bob. "That's it, Lofty. Phew! I think it must be time for lunch."

"Ooh, what have you got today, Bob?" asked Lofty.

"My favorite," said Bob happily. "Peanut butter and jelly sandwiches and a big cream puff."

When Bob opened his lunchbox, a gust of wind picked up his napkin.

"Quick Lofty," cried Bob. "It's blowing away."

They both raced off to catch the napkin. Bob's new boots squeaked noisily with each step.

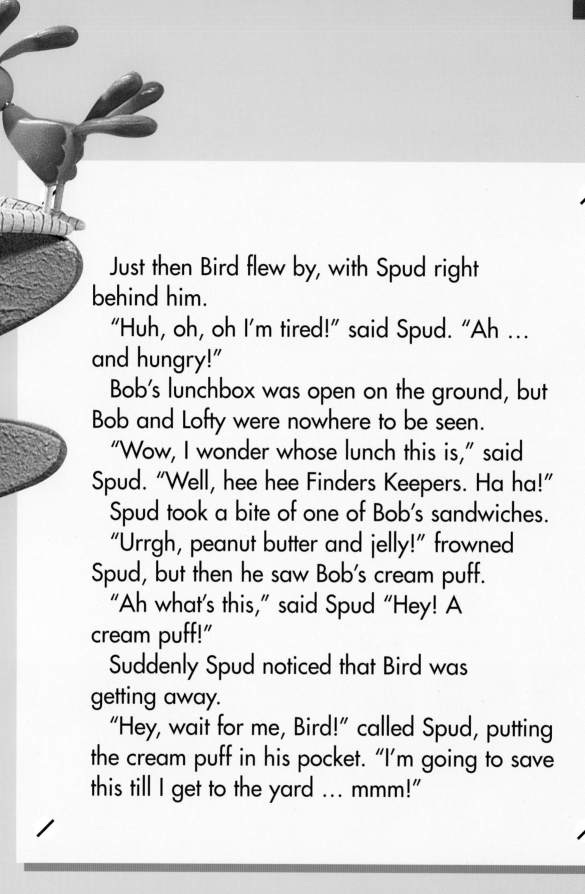

Just then Bird flew by, with Spud right behind him.

"Huh, oh, oh I'm tired!" said Spud. "Ah … and hungry!"

Bob's lunchbox was open on the ground, but Bob and Lofty were nowhere to be seen.

"Wow, I wonder whose lunch this is," said Spud. "Well, hee hee Finders Keepers. Ha ha!"

Spud took a bite of one of Bob's sandwiches.

"Urrgh, peanut butter and jelly!" frowned Spud, but then he saw Bob's cream puff.

"Ah what's this," said Spud "Hey! A cream puff!"

Suddenly Spud noticed that Bird was getting away.

"Hey, wait for me, Bird!" called Spud, putting the cream puff in his pocket. "I'm going to save this till I get to the yard … mmm!"

Bob and Lofty chased the napkin into a field where three little mice lived. The mice heard Bob's boots squeaking and started to follow him.

"Squeak squeak squeak!" said Bob's boots.

"Eek eek eek!" said the mice.

Finally, Bob caught the napkin.

"Ooh, phew," said Bob. "Got it Lofty. Ah, I'm ready for my lunch, after all that running around."

They headed back to Bob's lunchbox, but it was empty.

"Hold it, who's been eating my sandwiches?" cried Bob. "Where's my cream puff? Have you seen it Lofty?"

Just then, Lofty spotted the mice who were following Bob.

"Ooh arggghhh!" squealed Lofty. **"MICE!"**

"Mice?" asked Bob, confused. He turned around to look for the mice, but they ran behind him so he didn't see them.

Lofty was terrified, and sped off down the road toward the town.

"Come back Lofty," called Bob. "It isn't mice, it's only my boots."

Bob hurried off after Lofty, with the mice following behind his squeaky boots.

Lofty raced all the way to Bob's yard in a panic. Roley and Dizzy were there.

"Oh oh mice oh oh!" cried Lofty.

"Mice, Lofty? Where?" asked Dizzy.

Bob came running into the yard, with the mice still behind him.

"LOOK! M-MICE!" cried Lofty.

"Lofty, there aren't any mice, see?" said Bob.

He turned around to show Lofty, but this time he saw the mice.

"Ohh mice!" cried Bob, shocked. "Lofty, you were right!"

Bob walked around the yard and the mice followed close behind him.

"Ha ha. Look!" laughed Bob. "They like my squeaky boots, don't they?"

18

Just then, Bird arrived in Bob's yard and landed on Lofty. Spud came panting in behind him.

"Oh oh phew," sighed Spud. "Made it. All the way to Bob's Yard as the crow flies. Hee hee! Beat that, Bird!"

But Bird had already beaten him.

"Oh!" said Spud, disappointed. "Well, finally, I can have my cream puff."

He started to chomp happily on the cream puff and made such a mess that crumbs fell all over the ground. The mice ran over to eat them up.

"What have you got there, Spud?" asked Bob.

"Cream puff, Bob," mumbled Spud. "Er … oh … Is it yours?"

"Yes, it is mine," said Bob, annoyed. "You shouldn't take people's things without asking first."

"I didn't know Bob," said Spud. "I'm really sorry Bob."

The mice squeaked at Spud for more of his cream puff.

"Hey, get away, it's mine," cried Spud.

"Ha ha! Aren't you going to share it?" laughed Bob.

The mice chased Spud out of the yard, just as Wendy was coming in.

"Ha ha! Oh dear," said Wendy. "Where's Spud running off to?"

"Oh! … He's, he's just helping some friends get back home," laughed Bob.

"Bob, have you noticed?" said Wendy. "Your boots have stopped squeaking!"

"So they have," said Bob. "I must have broken them in with all that rushing around."

"You've had a busy day then?" asked Wendy. "Not really," replied Bob. "You could say it's been as quiet as a mouse!"

THE END!

Hinkler Books Pty Ltd 2004
17-23 Redwood Drive
Dingley, VIC 3172 Australia
www.hinklerbooks.com

© 2004 HIT Entertainment PLC and Keith Chapman
All rights reserved. Bob the Builder and all related logos and characters are trademarks
of HIT Entertainment PLC and Keith Chapman.
US edition published in 2002 by Simon Spotlight.

Bob's Boots - First published in the UK in 1998 by BBC Worldwide, Ltd.
Based on the script by Diane Redmond.
With thanks to HOT Animation.

ISBN: 1 8651 5982 4
Printed and bound in China